The Selfish Giant

by Oscar Wilde

Illustrated by
Katrien van der Grient

Floris Books

Every afternoon, as they were coming from school,
the children used to go and play in the Giant's garden.
It was a large lovely garden, with soft green grass.
Here and there over the grass stood beautiful flowers
like stars, and there were twelve peach-trees that in
spring-time broke out into delicate blossoms of pink
and pearl, and in autumn bore rich fruit. The birds sat
on the trees and sang so sweetly that the children used
to stop their games in order to listen to them.
"How happy we are here!" they cried to
each other.

One day the giant came back. He had
been to visit his friend, the Cornish ogre,
and had stayed with him for seven years.
After the seven years were over he had said
all he had to say, for his conversation was
limited, and he determined to return to his
own castle. When he arrived he saw the
children playing in the garden.
"What are you doing here?" he cried in
a very gruff voice, and the
children ran away.

"My own garden is my own garden," said the Giant; "any one can understand that, and I will allow nobody to play in it but myself." So he built a high wall round it, and put up a notice-board.

> TRESPASSERS WILL BE
> PROSECUTED

He was a very selfish Giant.

The poor children had now nowhere to play. They tried to play on the road, but the road was very dusty and full of hard stones, and they did not like it. They used to wander round the high walls when their lessons were over, and talk about the beautiful garden inside. "How happy we were there!" they said to each other.

Then the Spring came, and all over the country there were little blossoms and little birds. Only in the garden of the Selfish Giant it was still winter. The birds did not care to sing in it as there were no children, and the trees forgot to blossom. Once a beautiful flower put its head out of the grass, but when it saw the notice-board it was so sorry for the children that it slipped back into the ground again, and went off to sleep. The only people who were pleased were the Snow and the Frost. "Spring has forgotten this garden," they cried, "so we will live here all the year round." The Snow covered up the grass with her great white cloak, and the Frost painted all the trees silver.

Then they invited the North Wind to stay with them, and he came. He was wrapped in furs, and he roared all day about the garden, and blew the chimney pots down. "This is a delightful spot," he said, "we must ask the Hail on a visit."

So the Hail came. Every day for three hours he rattled on the roof of the castle till he broke most of the slates, and then he ran round and round the garden as fast as he could go. He was dressed in grey, and his breath was like ice.

"I cannot understand why the Spring is so late in coming," said the Selfish Giant, as he sat at the window and looked out at his cold, white garden; "I hope there will be a change in the weather."

But the Spring never came, nor the Summer. The Autumn gave golden fruit to every garden, but to the Giant's garden she gave none. "He is too selfish," she said. So it was always Winter there, and the North Wind and the Hail, and the Frost, and the Snow danced about through the trees.

One morning the Giant was lying awake in bed when he heard some lovely music. It sounded so sweet to his ears that he thought it must be the King's musicians passing by. It was really only a little linnet singing outside his window, but it was so long since he had heard a bird sing in his garden that it seemed to him to be the most beautiful music in the world. Then the Hail stopped dancing over his head, and the North Wind ceased roaring, and a delicious perfume came to him through the open casement. "I believe the Spring has come at last," said the Giant; and he jumped out of bed and looked out.

What did he see?

He saw a most wonderful sight. Through
a little hole in the wall the children had crept in, and they
were sitting in the branches of the trees. In every tree that
he could see there was a little child. And the trees were so
glad to have the children back again that they had covered
themselves with blossoms, and were waving their arms
gently above the children's heads.

The birds were flying about and twittering with delight, and the flowers were looking up through the green grass and laughing.

It was a lovely scene, only in one corner it was still winter. It was the farthest corner of the garden, and in it was standing a little boy. He was so small that he could not reach up to the branches of the tree, and he was wandering round it, crying bitterly. The poor tree was still covered with frost and snow, and the North Wind was blowing and roaring above it. "Climb up! little boy!" said the Tree, and it bent its branches down as low as it could; but the boy was too tiny.

And the Giant's heart melted as he looked out. "How selfish I have been!" he said; "now I know why the Spring would not come here. I will put that poor little boy on the top of the tree, and then I will knock down the wall, and my garden shall be the children's playground for ever and ever." He was really very sorry for what he had done.

So he crept downstairs and opened the front door quite softly, and went out into the garden. But when the children saw him they were so frightened that they all ran away, and the garden became winter again. Only the little boy did not run, for his eyes were so full of tears that he did not see the Giant coming. And the Giant stole up behind and took him gently in his hand, and put him up into the tree. And the tree broke at once into blossom, and the birds came and sang on it, and the little boy stretched out his two arms and flung them round the Giant's neck, and kissed him. And the other children when they saw that the Giant was not wicked any longer, came running back, and with them came the Spring.

"It is your garden now, little children," said the Giant, and he took a great axe and knocked down the wall. And when the people were going to market at twelve o'clock they found the Giant playing with the children in the most beautiful garden they had ever seen.

All day long they played, and in the evening they came to the Giant to bid him good-bye.

"But where is your little companion?" he said: "the boy I put into the tree?" The Giant loved him best because he had kissed him.

"We don't know," answered the children: "he has gone away."

"You must tell him to be sure and come tomorrow," said the Giant. But the children said that they did not know where he lived, and had never seen him before; and the Giant felt very sad.

Every afternoon, when school was over, the children came and played with the Giant. But the little boy whom the Giant loved was never seen again. The Giant was very kind to all the children, yet he longed for his little friend and often spoke of him. "How I would like to see him!" he used to say.

Years went over, and the Giant grew very old and feeble. He could not play about any more, so he sat in a huge arm-chair, and watched the children at their games, and admired his garden. "I have many beautiful flowers," he said: "but the children are the most beautiful flowers of all."

One winter morning he looked out of his window as he was dressing. He did not hate Winter now, for he knew that it was merely the Spring asleep, and that the flowers were resting.

Suddenly he rubbed his eyes in wonder and looked and looked. It certainly was a marvellous sight. In the farthest corner of the garden was a tree quite covered with lovely white blossoms. Its branches were golden, and the silver fruit hung down from them, and underneath it stood the boy he had loved.

Downstairs ran the Giant in great
joy, and out into the garden. He hastened
across the grass, and came near to the child. And
when he came quite close his face grew red with anger,
and he said, "Who hath dared to wound thee?" For on
the palms of the child's hands were the prints of two
nails, and the prints of two nails were on the little feet.

"Who hath dared to wound thee?" cried the Giant;
"tell me, that I may take my big sword and slay him."

"Nay!" answered the child: "but these are the
wounds of Love."

"Who art thou?" said the Giant, and a strange awe
fell on him, and he knelt before the little child.
And the child smiled on the Giant, and
said to him, "You let me play once in
your garden, today you shall come
with me to my garden, which is
Paradise."

And when the children ran in that afternoon, they found the Giant lying dead under the tree, all covered with white blossom.